K!
BOUT
MY
TUMMY ACHE!

The Great Sphinx,
at one time painted red and yellow,
has the head of a pharaoh and
the body of a lion—making it

THE MANE MAN OF EGYPT

WHAT
SNAPPY
DRESSERS!

Want to know how big the Great Pyramid really is?
If you broke the Great Pyramid into rods about
2 1/2 inches square and joined them together
into one long rod, you could climb
all the way to the moon. Of course, a

ROCKET SHIP

would get you there faster!

The Nile, the world's longest river,
was the main highway
for ancient Egypt.
That must have made hitchhiking

AWFULLY
DIFFICULT.

Thirty times larger than
the Empire State
Building, the Great
Pyramid of Giza
can be seen from the

MOON.

FACTS

TEN LITTLE MUMMIES

AN EGYPTIAN COUNTING BOOK

BY
PHILIP YATES
ILLUSTRATED BY
G. BRIAN KARAS

VIKING

VIKING

Published by Penguin Group
Penguin Young Readers Group, 345 Hudson Street, New York, New York 10014, U.S.A.
Penguin Books Ltd, 80 Strand, London WC2R 0RL, England
Penguin Books Australia Ltd, 250 Camberwell Road, Camberwell, Victoria 3124, Australia
Penguin Books Canada Ltd, 10 Alcorn Avenue, Toronto, Ontario, Canada M4V 3B2
Penguin Books (N.Z.) Ltd, 182-190 Wairau Road, Auckland 10, New Zealand

First published in 2003 by Viking, a division of Penguin Young Readers Group.

1 3 5 7 9 10 8 6 4 2

LIBRARY OF CONGRESS CATALOGING-IN-PUBLICATION DATA
Yates, Philip.
Ten little mummies : an Egyptian counting book / by Philip Yates ; illustrated by G. Brian Karas.
p. cm.
Summary: Ten little mummies become bored with staying in a room together
all day but when they go outside to play they disappear, one by one.
ISBN 0-670-03641-2 (hardcover)
[1. Mummies—Fiction. 2. Egypt—Fiction. 3. Counting. 4. Stories in rhyme.]
I. Karas, G. Brian, ill. II. Title.
PZ8.3.Y37 Te 2003   [E]–dc21   2002155491

Manufactured in China
Set in Kabel
Book design by Teresa Kietlinski

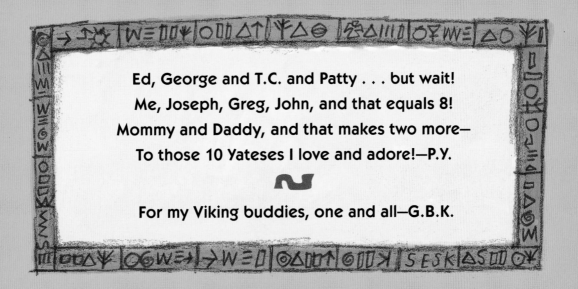

DEEP UNDERGROUND

IN A DREARY OLD TOMB,

10

little mummies were stuffed
in one room.
Nothing to play with,
no books on the shelves,
just ten little mummies
WRAPPED UP
in themselves.

"This is the pits!"
said a mummy one day.
"I am bored stiff—
let's go outside and

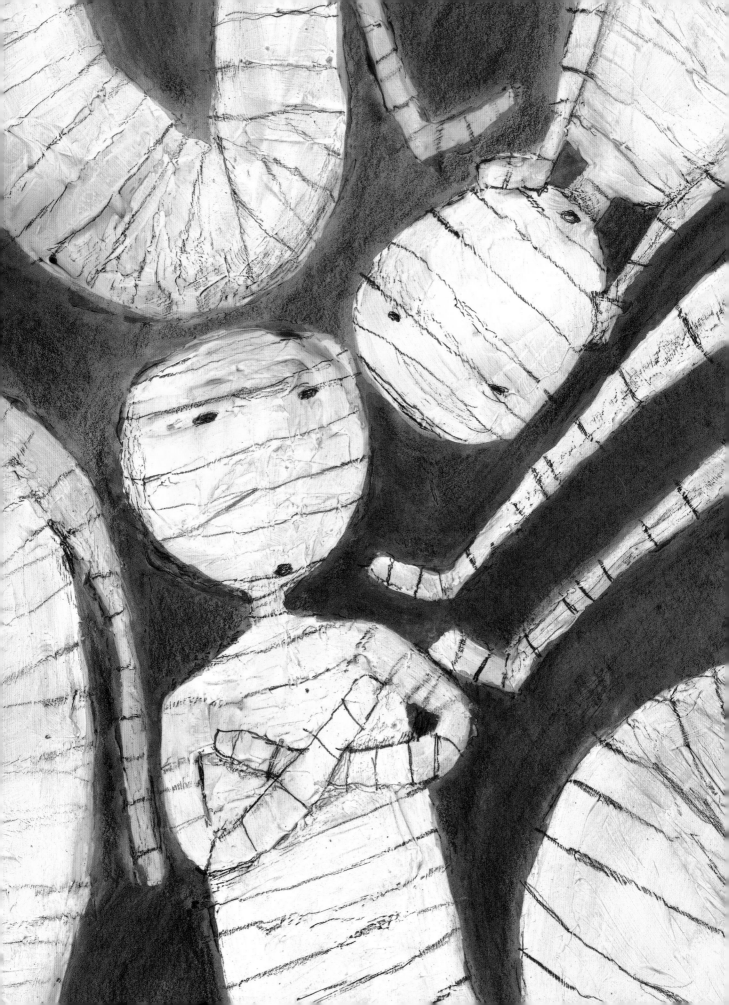

10 little mummies
went out to have fun.
One suffered
HEAT STROKE
and ran from the sun.

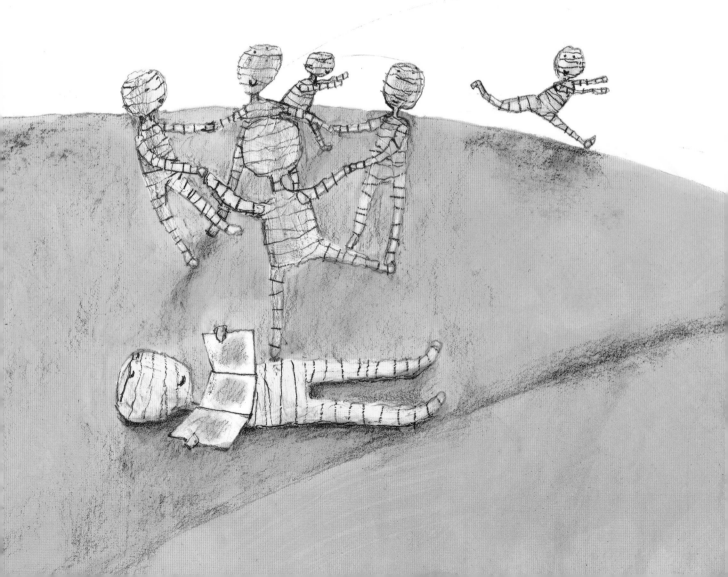

9 little mummies dove
into the NILE.
One swam away
from a

BIG CROCODILE.

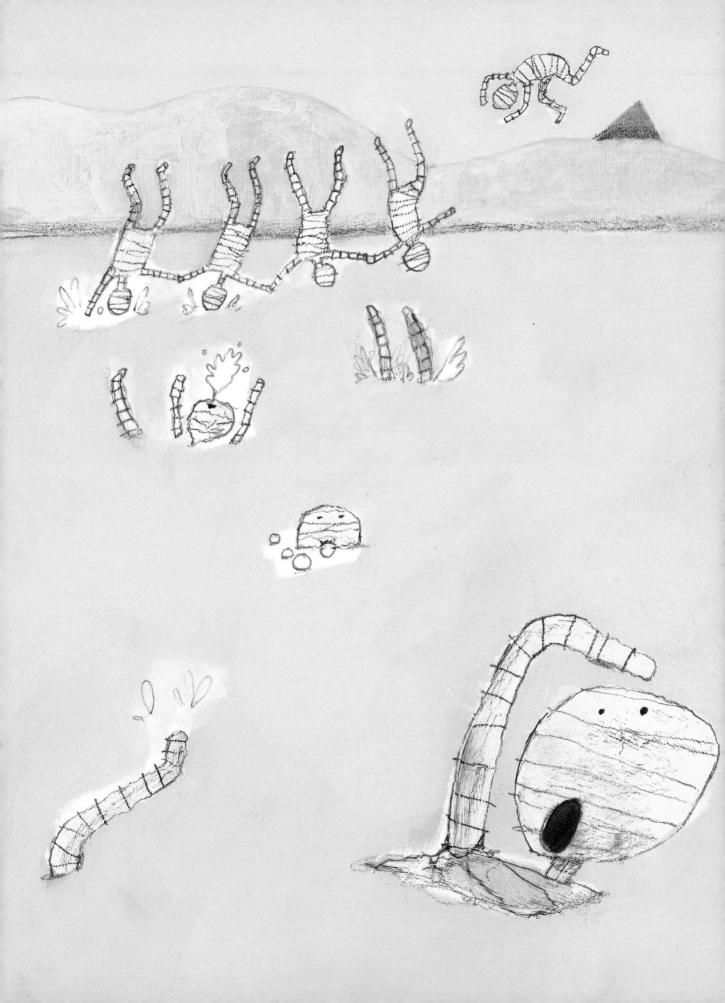

8 little mummies
committed hijinks.
One was arrested for painting the
SPHINX.

7 little mummies
got lost in the dunes.
One was adopted by friendly
BABOONS.

6 little mummies
raced over the plains.
One lost CONTROL
of his chariot's reins.

5 little mummies
climbed fifty feet high.
One DISAPPEARED
when a falcon
swooped by.

4 little mummies yelled,

"PYRAMID SLIDE!"

One came
unraveled
and snuck off
to hide.

3 little mummies played desert croquet.

WHOOSH!

went a sandstorm and blew one away.

2 little mummies
went hunting that night.
One roped a HIPPO,
then rode out of sight.

1

lonely mummy
with tears in her eyes
opened the door of the tomb
and—

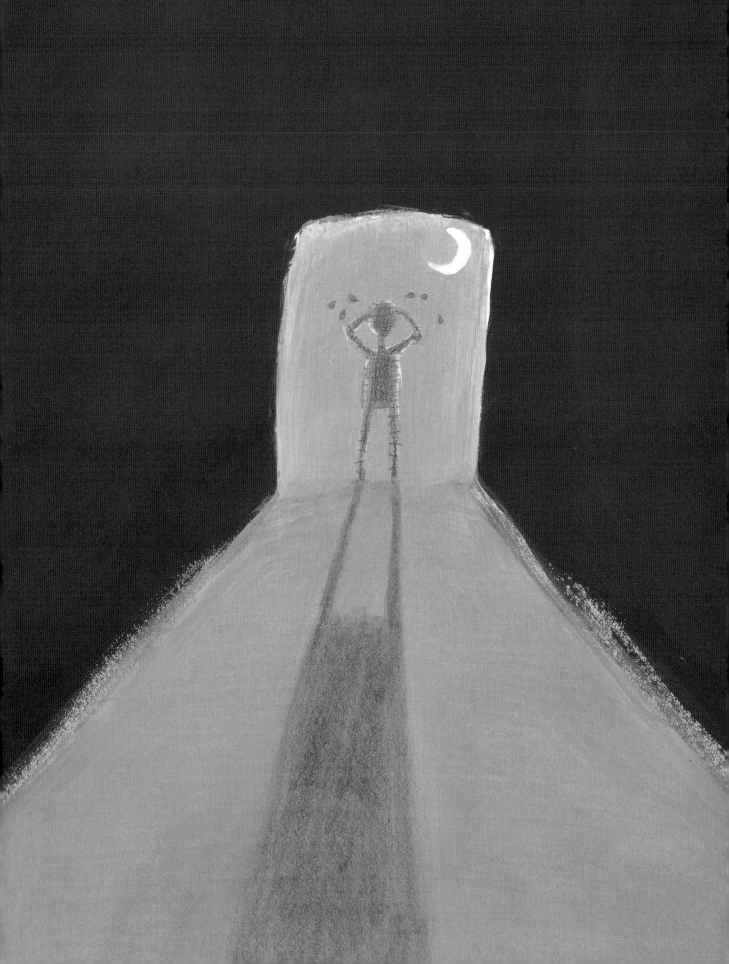

"SURPRISE!"

There in the dark
with their faces aglow,
9
little mummies
all stood in a row!

9

little mummies

and **1** more is **10**.

10

little mummies

TOGETHER AGAIN!

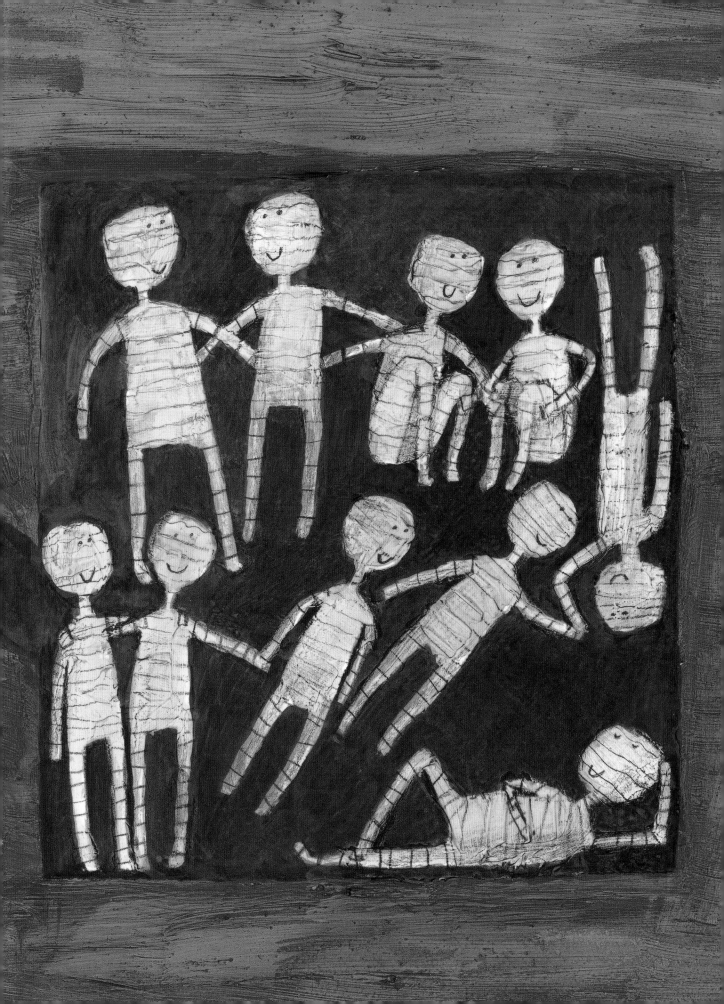

10 little mummies'
adventures are done.

Let's hope tomorrow is twice as much **FUN!**

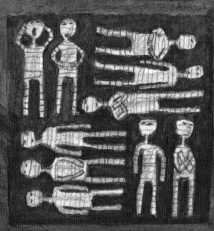

In the Middle Ages, people used to chop up mummies and use them as medicine for sick people.

The tomb of King Tut was discovered with 3,000-year-old treasures including over 300 articles of clothing and 200 pieces of jewelry, about 100 baskets of food, 4 game boards, 3 trumpets, 6 war chariots, 35 model boats, and furniture. Now that's the kind of tomb you wouldn't mind being

CAUGHT DEAD IN!

Discovered by Howard Carter in 1922, the contents of King Tut's tomb are now in the Cairo Museum. It took Carter nearly ten years to empty Tut's tomb . . . and another five

JUST TO UNWIND!

Crocodiles in Egypt were worshipped as gods and mummified wearing golden earrings and bracelets.

The ancient Egyptians trained baboons to climb date trees and bring the fruit back to the Pharaohs. It's never too late to train your

PARENTS!

The Great Pyramid at Giza stood more than 480 feet tall and contained over 2.5 million blocks of stone. The stones weigh from two to fifty tons!

AREN'T YOU GLAD YOU DIDN'T HAVE TO CARRY ANY?

ANCIENT EGYPT